BARN DANCE!

By Bill Martin Jr.
and John Archambault

Illustrated by Ted Rand

A TRUMPET CLUB SPECIAL EDITION

Full moon shinin', shinin' big an' bright,
Pushin' back the shadows, holdin' back the night.
Not a thing stirrin', quiet as could be,
Just the whisper of the leaves on the cottonwood tree.

Ol' houn' dog, whinin' in his sleep,
Dreamin' after rabbits in a game of hide 'n seek.
Over in the farmhouse, all the lights were out,
Farmer an' his wife an' kids, not a one about—

All except the skinny kid with questions in his head,
Much too full of wonderment to spend the night in bed,
He was up about an' list'nin'. . .

. . . when the night owl said,
Come a little closer . . .
Come a little closer . . .
Listen to the night . . .
There's magic in the air . . . .

Then the skinny kid heard it . . . heard it faint begin . . .
A *plink! plink! plink!* on the wind's violin . . .
Comin' from the corn field . . . sweet 'n soft 'n low . . .
Music honeyed up by the ol' scarecrow . . .
A-plinkin' on the fiddle strings to tune 'em up just so . . . .

The scarecrow tucked the fiddle underneath his chin
An' fiddled out a welcome to all his country kin.
He fiddled through the woods 'n fields 'n all aroun' the farm,
Biddin' ever'body come to a hoedown in the barn.

There was so much chit 'n chatter when the critters all arrived,
That no one saw the skinny kid oozle in an' hide
Just in time to hear the crow call the dance, *Begin!*
Grab yourself a partner an' jump right in!

Right hand! Left hand! Around you go!
Now back-to-back your partner in a do-si-do!
Mules to the center for a curtsey an' a bow!
An' hey there, skinny kid! Show the old cow how!

Out came the skinny kid, a-tickin' an' a-tockin'
An' a hummin' an' a-yeein' an' a-rockin' an' a-sockin'.
An' he danced his little toe through a hole in his stockin'!

He leaped the apple barrel an' the pun'kins in a pile,
An' he showed 'em how to wagon-wheel, barnyard style.
Now rocket to the moon an' powder-puff your noses,
An' hurry home to mama on your little pink toeses!

Five times! Ten times! Fifteen! Twenty!
Now spin once again an' that's a-plenty!
But the fat little pigs whirled 'round 'n 'round,
'Till they got so dizzy that they all fell down.

The sky was warmin' up for the comin' of the day
When the skinny kid . . . heard . . . the night owl . . . say,

Mornin's comin' closer . . .
Mornin's comin' closer . . .
The magic time is over . . .
Night'll soon be gone . . . .

The ol' dog stretched 'n blinked a sleepy eye
Just a blink too late to see the skinny kid slip by . . .

He tiptoed through the kitchen . . . an' tiptoed up the stairs . . .
As quiet as a feather . . . on a breath of air . . . .

He hummed a little do-si-do an' flopped himself in bed . . .
With the wonders of the barn dance . . . dancin' in his head.

For my father, Virgil Archambault,
first of Terrebonne, Minnesota,
and now of Sierra Madre, California,
a born barn dancer in step and spirit.

John Archambault

Published by The Trumpet Club
666 Fifth Avenue, New York, New York 10103

ISBN: 0-440-84453-3

This edition published by arrangement with
Henry Holt and Company, Inc.
Printed in the United States of America
October 1990

10 9 8 7 6 5 4 3
UPC